What's the time, Mr Wolf?

What's the time, Mr Wolf?

**FONTANA
PICTURE LIONS**

First published in Great Britain 1983 by William Heinemann Ltd
First published in this edition by Picture Lions 1986
8 Grafton Street, London W1X 3LA
Picture Lions is an imprint of Fontana Paperbacks,
a division of the Collins Publishing Group
Copyright © Colin Hawkins 1983, 1986
Printed in Great Britain
by William Collins Sons & Co. Ltd, Glasgow

What's the time, Mr Wolf?

What's the time, Mr Wolf?

What's the time, Mr Wolf?

What's the time, Mr Wolf?

What's the time,
Mr Wolf?

What's the time, Mr Wolf?

What's the time, Mr Wolf?

What's the time, Mr Wolf?